W9-BRM-745

This book belongs to

_____

THE TALE OF
PETER RABBIT
AND OTHER STORIES BY
BEATRIX POTTER

THE TALE OF PETER RABBIT

AND OTHER STORIES BY
BEATRIX POTTER

ILLUSTRATED BY
ALLEN ATKINSON

ALFRED A. KNOPF   NEW YORK   1984

THIS IS A BORZOI BOOK
PUBLISHED BY ALFRED A. KNOPF, INC.
Copyright © 1982 by Armand Eisen
All rights reserved under International and
Pan-American Copyright Conventions.
Published in the United States by Alfred A. Knopf, Inc., New York.
Distributed by Random House, Inc., New York.

Published April 3, 1983
Reprinted Once
Third Printing, February 1984

Potter, Beatrix. [date]
The tale of Peter Rabbit and other stories.

   Summary: The classic tales of Peter Rabbit, Squirrel
Nutkin, Mrs. Tiggy-Winkle, the Tailor of Gloucester, Jeremy
Fisher, Benjamin Bunny, Miss Moppet, and the Two Bad Mice,
plus Apply Dappley's Nursery Rhymes, with new illustrations.
   1. Children's stories, English. [1. Animals—Fiction. 2.
Short stories] I. Atkinson, Allen, ill. II. Title.
PZ7.P85Tag 1982   [E]   82-47808
ISBN 0-394-52845-X

The artwork for this edition is dedicated
to my parents, Robert and Pearl Gunther,
and to the memory of my father,
John Atkinson.

CONTENTS

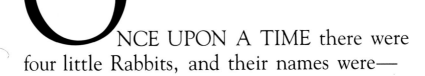

ONCE UPON A TIME there were four little Rabbits, and their names were—

Flopsy, Mopsy, Cotton-tail,   and Peter.

They lived with their Mother in a sand-bank, underneath the root of a very big fir-tree.

"Now, my dears," said old Mrs. Rabbit one morning, "you may go into the fields or down the lane, but don't go into Mr. McGregor's garden: your Father had an accident there; he was put in a pie by Mrs. McGregor.

"Now run along, and don't get into mischief. I am going out."

Then old Mrs. Rabbit took a basket and her umbrella, and went through the wood to the baker's. She bought a loaf of brown bread and five currant buns.

Flopsy, Mopsy, and Cotton-tail, who were good little bunnies, went down the lane to gather blackberries:

15

But Peter, who was very naughty, ran straight away to Mr. McGregor's garden, and squeezed under the gate!

First he ate some lettuces and some French beans; and then he ate some radishes;

And then, feeling rather sick, he went to look for some parsley.

THE TALE OF PETER RABBIT

But round the end of a cucumber frame, whom should he meet but Mr. McGregor!

Mr. McGregor was on his hands and knees planting out young cabbages, but he jumped up and ran after Peter, waving a rake and calling out, "Stop thief!"

Peter was most dreadfully frightened; he rushed all over the garden, for he had forgotten the way back to the gate.

He lost one of his shoes among the cabbages, and the other shoe amongst the potatoes.

After losing them, he ran on four legs and

went faster, so that I think he might have got away altogether if he had not unfortunately run into a gooseberry net, and got caught by the large buttons on his jacket. It was a blue jacket with brass buttons, quite new.

Peter gave himself up for lost, and shed big tears; but his sobs were overheard by some friendly sparrows, who flew to him in great excitement, and implored him to exert himself.

Mr. McGregor came up with a sieve, which he intended to pop upon the top of Peter; but Peter wriggled out just in time, leaving his jacket behind him.

And rushed into the tool-shed, and jumped into a can. It would have been a beautiful thing to hide in, if it had not had so much water in it.

Mr. McGregor was quite sure that Peter was somewhere in the tool-shed, perhaps hidden underneath a flower-pot. He began to turn them over carefully, looking under each.

Presently Peter sneezed—"Kertyschoo!" Mr. McGregor was after him in no time.

And tried to put his foot upon Peter, who jumped out of a window, upsetting three plants. The window was too small for Mr. McGregor, and he was tired of running after Peter. He went back to his work.

Peter sat down to rest; he was out of breath and trembling with fright, and he had not the least idea which way to go. Also he was very damp with sitting in that can.

After a time he began to wander about, going lippity—lippity—not very fast, and looking all round.

He found a door in a wall; but it was locked, and there was no room for a fat little rabbit to squeeze underneath.

An old mouse was running in and out over the stone door-step, carrying peas and beans to her family in the wood. Peter asked her the way to the gate, but she had such a large pea in her mouth that she could not answer. She only shook her head at him. Peter began to cry.

Then he tried to find his way straight across the garden, but he became more and more puzzled. Presently, he came to a pond where Mr. McGregor filled his water-cans. A white cat was staring at some gold-fish, she sat very, very still, but now and then the tip of her tail twitched as if it were alive. Peter thought it best to go away without speaking to her; he had heard about cats from his cousin, little Benjamin Bunny.

He went back towards the tool-shed, but suddenly, quite close to him, he heard the noise of a hoe—scr-r-ritch, scratch, scratch, scritch. Peter scuttered underneath the bushes. But presently, as nothing happened, he came out, and climbed upon a wheelbarrow and peeped over. The first thing he saw was Mr. McGregor hoeing onions. His back was turned towards Peter, and beyond him was the gate!

Peter got down very quietly off the wheelbarrow, and started running as fast as he could go, along a straight walk behind some black-currant bushes.

Mr. McGregor caught sight of him at the corner, but Peter did not care. He slipped underneath the gate, and was safe at last in the wood outside the garden.

Mr. McGregor hung up the little jacket and the shoes for a scare-crow to frighten the blackbirds.

Peter never stopped running or

looked behind him till he got home to the big fir-tree.

He was so tired that he flopped down upon the nice soft sand on the floor of the rabbit-hole and shut his eyes. His mother was busy cooking; she wondered what he had done with his clothes. It was the second little jacket and pair of shoes that Peter had lost in a fortnight!

I am sorry to say that Peter was not very well during the evening.

His mother put him to bed, and made some camomile tea; and she gave a dose of it to Peter!

"One table-spoonful to be taken at bed-time."

But Flopsy, Mopsy, and Cotton-tail had bread and milk and blackberries for supper.

THE TAILOR OF GLOUCESTER

IN THE TIME of swords and periwigs and full-skirted coats with flowered lappets—when gentlemen wore ruffles, and gold-laced waistcoats of paduasoy and taffeta—there lived a tailor in Gloucester.

He sat in the window of a little shop in Westgate Street, cross-legged on a table, from morning till dark.

All day long while the light lasted he sewed and snippeted, piecing out his satin and pompadour, and lutestring; stuffs had strange names, and were very expensive in the days of the Tailor of Gloucester.

But although he sewed fine silk for his neighbours, he himself was very, very poor—a little old man in spectacles, with a pinched face, old crooked fingers, and a suit of thread-bare clothes.

He cut his coats without waste, according to his embroidered cloth; they were very small ends and snippets that lay about upon the table—"Too narrow breadths for nought—except waistcoats for mice," said the tailor.

One bitter cold day near Christmas-time the tailor began to make a coat—a coat of cherry-coloured corded silk embroidered with pansies and roses, and a cream-coloured satin waistcoat—trimmed with gauze and green worsted chenille—for the Mayor of Gloucester.

The tailor worked and worked, and he talked to himself. He measured the silk, and turned it round and round, and trimmed it into shape with his shears; the table was all littered with cherry-coloured snippets.

"No breadth at all, and cut on the cross; it is no breadth at all; tippets for mice and ribbons for mobs! for mice!" said the Tailor of Gloucester.

When the slow-flakes came down against the small leaded window-panes and shut out the light, the tailor had done his day's work; all the silk and satin lay cut out upon the table.

There were twelve pieces for the coat and four pieces for the waistcoat; and there were pocket flaps and cuffs, and buttons all in order. For the lining of the coat there was fine yellow taffeta; and for the button-holes of the waistcoat, there was cherry-coloured twist. And everything was ready to sew together in the morning, all measured and sufficient—except that there was wanting just one single skein of cherry-coloured twisted silk.

The tailor came out of his shop at dark, for he did not sleep there at nights; he fastened the window and locked the door, and took away the key. No one lived there at night but little brown mice, and they run in and out without any keys!

For behind the wooden wainscots of all the old houses in Gloucester, there are little mouse staircases and secret trap-doors; and the mice run from house to house through those long narrow passages; they can run all over the town without going into the streets.

But the tailor came out of his shop, and shuffled home through the snow. He lived quite near by in College Court, next the doorway to College Green; and although it was not a big house, the tailor was so poor he only rented the kitchen.

He lived alone with his cat; it was called Simpkin.

Now all day long while the tailor was out at work, Simpkin kept house by himself; and he also was fond of the mice, though he gave them no satin for coats!

"Miaw?" said the cat when the tailor opened the door. "Miaw?"

The tailor replied—"Simpkin, we shall make our fortune, but I am worn to a ravelling. Take this groat (which is our last fourpence) and Simpkin, take a china pipkin; buy a penn'orth of bread, a penn'orth of milk and a penn'orth of sausages. And oh, Simpkin, with the last penny of our fourpence buy me one penn'orth of cherry-coloured silk. But do not lose the last penny of the fourpence, Simpkin, or I am undone and worn to a thread-paper, for I have NO MORE TWIST."

Then Simpkin again said, "Miaw?" and took the groat and the pipkin, and went out into the dark.

The tailor was very tired and beginning to be ill. He sat down by the hearth and talked to himself about that wonderful coat.

"I shall make my fortune—to be cut bias—
the Mayor of Gloucester is to be married on
Christmas Day in the morning, and he hath ordered
a coat and an embroidered waistcoat—to be lined
with yellow taffeta—and the taffeta sufficeth; there
is no more left over in snippets than will serve to
make tippets for mice—"

Then the tailor started; for suddenly,
interrupting him, from the dresser at the other side
of the kitchen came a number of little noises—

Tip tap, tip tap, tip tap tip!

"Now what can that be?" said the Tailor of
Gloucester, jumping up from his chair. The dresser
was covered with crockery and pipkins, willow
pattern plates, and tea-cups and mugs.

The tailor crossed the kitchen, and stood
quite still beside the dresser, listening, and peering
through his spectacles. Again from under a tea-cup,
came those funny little noises—

Tip tap, tip tap, tip tap tip!

"This is very peculiar,"
said the Tailor of Gloucester;
and he lifted up the tea-cup
which was upside down.

Out stepped a little live lady mouse, and made a curtsey to the tailor! Then she hopped away down off the dresser, and under the wainscot.

The tailor sat down again by the fire, warming his poor cold hands, and mumbling to himself—

"The waistcoat is cut out from peach-coloured satin—tambour stitch and rose-buds in beautiful floss silk. Was I wise to entrust my last fourpence to Simpkin? One-and-twenty button-holes of cherry-coloured twist!"

But all at once, from the dresser, there came other little noises:

Tip tap, tip tap, tip tap tip!

"This is passing extraordinary!"
said the Tailor of Gloucester, and
turned over another tea-cup, which
was upside down.

Out stepped a little gentle
man mouse, and made a bow to
the tailor!

And then from all over the
dresser came a chorus of little tappings,
all sounding together, and answering one another,
like watch-beetles in an old worm-eaten window-
shutter—

Tip tap, tip tap, tip tap tip!

And out from under tea-cups and from under
bowls and basins, stepped other and more little mice
who hopped away down off the dresser and under
the wainscot.

The tailor sat down, close over the fire, lamenting—"One-and-twenty button-holes of cherry-coloured silk! To be finished by noon of Saturday: and this is Tuesday evening. Was it right to let loose those mice, undoubtedly the property of Simpkin? Alack, I am undone, for I have no more twist!"

The little mice came out again, and listened to the tailor; they took notice of the pattern of that wonderful coat. They whispered to one another about the taffeta lining, and about little mouse tippets.

And then all at once they all ran away together down the passage behind the wainscot, squeaking and calling to one another, as they ran from house to house; and not one mouse was left in the tailor's kitchen when Simpkin came back with the pipkin of milk!

Simpkin opened the door and bounced in, with an angry "G-r-r-miaw!" like a cat that is vexed: for he hated the snow, and there was snow in his ears, and snow in his collar at the back of his neck. He put down the loaf and the sausages upon the dresser, and sniffed.

"Simpkin," said the tailor, "where is my twist?"

But Simpkin set down the pipkin of milk upon the dresser, and looked suspiciously at the tea-cups. He wanted his supper of little fat mouse!

"Simpkin," said the tailor, "where is my TWIST?"

But Simpkin hid a little parcel privately in the tea-pot, and spit and growled at the tailor; and if Simpkin had been able to talk, he would have asked: "Where is my MOUSE?"

"Alack, I am undone!" said the Tailor of Gloucester, and went sadly to bed.

All that night long Simpkin hunted and searched through the kitchen, peeping into cupboards and under the wainscot, and into the tea-pot where he had hidden that twist; but still he found never a mouse!

Whenever the tailor muttered and talked in his sleep, Simpkin said "Miaw-ger-r-w-s-s-ch!" and made strange horrid noises, as cats do at night.

For the poor old tailor was very ill with a fever, tossing and turning in his four-post bed; and still in his dreams he mumbled—"No more twist! No more twist!"

All that day he was ill, and the next day, and the next; and what should become of the cherry-coloured coat? In the tailor's shop in Westgate Street the embroidered silk and satin lay cut out upon the table—one-and-twenty button-holes—and who should come to sew them, when the window was barred, and the door was fast locked?

But that does not hinder the little brown mice; they run in and out without any keys through all the old houses in Gloucester!

Out of doors the market folks went trudging through the snow to buy their geese and turkeys, and to bake their Christmas pies; but there would be no Christmas dinner for Simpkin and the poor old Tailor of Gloucester.

The tailor lay ill for three days and nights; and then it was Christmas Eve, and very late at night. The moon climbed up over the roofs and chimneys, and looked down over the gateway into College Court. There were no lights in the

windows, nor any sound in the houses; all the city of Gloucester was fast asleep under the snow.

And still Simpkin wanted his mice, and he mewed as he stood beside the four-post bed.

But it is in the old story that all the beasts can talk, in the night between Christmas Eve and Christmas Day in the morning (though there are very few folk that can hear them, or know what it is that they say).

When the Cathedral clock struck twelve there was an answer—like an echo of the chimes—and Simpkin heard it, and came out of the tailor's door, and wandered about in the snow.

From all the roofs and gables and old wooden houses in Gloucester came a thousand merry voices singing the old Christmas rhymes—all the old songs that ever I heard of, and some that I don't know, like Whittington's bells.

First and loudest the cocks cried out: "Dame, get up, and bake your pies!"

"Oh, dilly, dilly, dilly!" sighed Simpkin.

And now in a garret there were lights and sounds of dancing, and cats came from over the way.

"Hey, diddle, diddle, the cat and the fiddle! All the cats in Gloucester—except me," said Simpkin.

Under the wooden eaves the starlings and sparrows sang of Christmas pies; the jack-daws woke up in the Cathedral tower; and although it was the middle of the night the throstles and robins sang; the air was quite full of little twittering tunes.

But it was all rather provoking to poor hungry Simpkin!

Particularly he was vexed with some little shrill voices from behind a wooden lattice. I think that they were bats, because they always have very small voices—especially in a black frost, when they talk in their sleep, like the Tailor of Gloucester.

They said something mysterious that sounded like—

"Buz, quoth the blue fly; hum, quoth the bee;
Buz and hum they cry, and so do we!"

and Simpkin went away shaking his ears as if he had a bee in his bonnet.

From the tailor's shop in Westgate came a glow of light; and when Simpkin crept up to peep in at the window it was full of candles. There was a

snippeting of scissors, and snappeting of thread; and
little mouse voices sang loudly and gaily—

"Four-and-twenty tailors
Went to catch a snail,
The best man amongst them
Durst not touch her tail;
She put out her horns
Like a little kyloe cow,
Run, tailors, run! or she'll have you all e'en now!"

Then without a pause the little mouse voices
went on again—

"Sieve my lady's oatmeal,
Grind my lady's flour,
Put it in a chestnut,
Let it stand an hour—"

"Mew! Mew!" interrupted Simpkin, and he scratched at the door. But the key was under the tailor's pillow, he could not get in.

The little mice only laughed, and tried another tune—

"Three little mice sat down to spin,
Pussy passed by and she peeped in.
What are you at, my fine little men?
Making coats for gentlemen.
Shall I come in and cut off your threads?
Oh, no, Miss Pussy, you'd bite off our heads!"

"Mew! Mew!" cried Simpkin. "Hey diddle dinketty?" answered the little mice—

"Hey diddle dinketty, poppetty pet!
The merchants of London they wear scarlet;
Silk in the collar, and gold in the hem,
So merrily march the merchantmen!"

They clicked their thimbles to mark the time, but none of the songs pleased Simpkin; he sniffed and mewed at the door of the shop.

"And then I bought
A pipkin and a popkin,
A slipkin and a slopkin,
All for one farthing—

and upon the kitchen dresser!" added the rude little mice.

"Mew! scratch! scratch!" scuffled Simpkin on the window-sill; while the little mice inside sprang to their feet, and all began to shout at once in little twittering voices: "No more twist! No more twist!" And they barred up the window shutters and shut out Simpkin.

But still through the nicks in the shutters he could hear the click of thimbles, and little mouse voices singing—

"No more twist! No more twist!"

Simpkin came away from the shop and went home, considering in his mind. He found the poor old tailor without fever, sleeping peacefully.

Then Simpkin went on tip-toe and took a little parcel of silk out of the tea-pot, and looked at it in the moonlight; and he felt quite ashamed of his badness compared with those good little mice!

When the tailor awoke in the morning, the first thing which he saw upon the patchwork quilt, was a skein of cherry-coloured twisted silk, and beside his bed stood the repentant Simpkin!

"Alack, I am worn to a ravelling," said the Tailor of Gloucester, "but I have my twist!"

The sun was shining on the snow when the tailor got up and dressed, and came out into the street with Simpkin running before him.

The starlings whistled on the chimney stacks, and the throstles and robins sang—but they sang their own little noises, not the words they had sung in the night.

"Alack," said the tailor, "I have my twist; but no more strength—nor time—than will serve to make me one single button-hole; for this is Christmas Day in the Morning! The Mayor of Gloucester shall be married by noon—and where is his cherry-coloured coat?"

He unlocked the door of the little shop in Westgate Street, and Simpkin ran in, like a cat that expects something.

But there was no one there! Not even one little brown mouse!

The boards were swept clean; the little ends of thread and the little silk snippets were all tidied away, and gone from off the floor.

But upon the table—oh joy! the tailor gave a shout—there, where he had left plain cuttings of silk—there lay the most beautifullest coat and embroidered satin waistcoat that ever were worn by a Mayor of Gloucester.

There were roses and pansies upon the facings of the coat; and the waistcoat was worked with poppies and corn-flowers.

Everything was finished except just one single cherry-coloured button-hole, and where that button-hole was wanting there was pinned a scrap of paper with these words—in little teeny weeny writing—

NO MORE TWIST

And from then began the luck of the Tailor of Gloucester; he grew quite stout, and he grew quite rich.

He made the most wonderful waistcoats for all the rich merchants of Gloucester, and for all the fine gentlemen of the country round.

Never were seen such ruffles, or such embroidered cuffs and lappets! But his button-holes were the greatest triumph of it all.

The stitches of those button-holes were so neat—*so* neat—I wonder how they could be stitched by an old man in spectacles, with crooked old fingers, and a tailor's thimble.

The stitches of those button-holes were so small—*so* small—they looked as if they had been made by little mice!

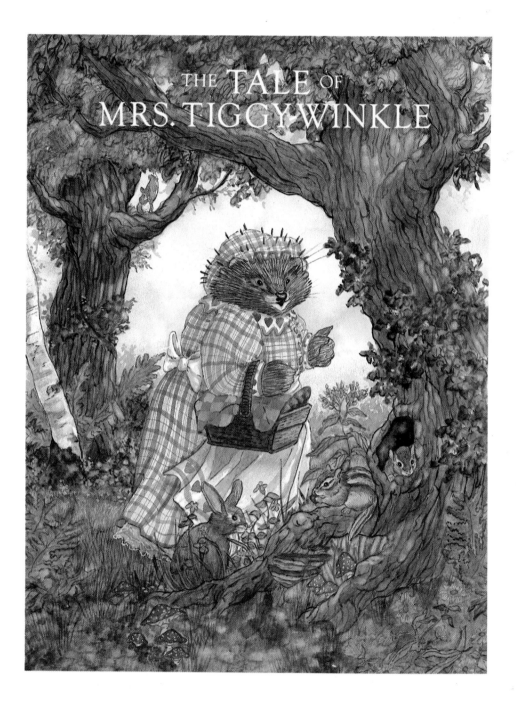

THE TALE OF
MRS. TIGGY-WINKLE

ONCE UPON A TIME there was a little girl called Lucie, who lived at a farm called Little-town. She was a good little girl—only she was always losing her pocket-handkerchiefs!

One day little Lucie came into the farm-yard crying—oh, she did cry so! "I've lost my pocket-handkin! Three handkins and a pinny! Have *you* seen them, Tabby Kitten?"

The Kitten went on washing her white paws; so Lucie asked a speckled hen—

"Sally Henny-penny, have *you* found three pocket-handkins?"

But the speckled hen ran into a barn, clucking —"I go barefoot, barefoot, barefoot!"

And then Lucie asked Cock Robin sitting on a twig.

Cock Robin looked sideways at Lucie with his bright black eye, and he flew over a stile and away.

Lucie climbed upon the stile and looked up at the hill behind Little-town —a hill that goes up— up—

49

into the clouds as though it had no top!

And a great way up the hill-side she thought she saw some white things spread upon the grass.

Lucie scrambled up the hill as fast as her stout legs would carry her; she ran along a steep path-way—up and up—until Little-town was right away down below—she could have dropped a pebble down the chimney!

Presently she came to a spring, bubbling out from the hill-side.

Some one had stood a tin can upon a stone to catch the water—but the water was already running over, for the can was no bigger than an egg-cup! And where the sand upon the path was wet—there were foot-marks of a *very* small person.

Lucie ran on, and on.

The path ended under a big rock. The grass was short and green, and there were clothes-props

cut from bracken stems, with lines of plaited rushes, and a heap of tiny clothes pins—but no pocket-handkerchiefs!

But there was something else—a door! straight into the hill; and inside it some one was singing—

"Lily-white and clean, oh!
With little frills between, oh!
Smooth and hot—red rusty spot
Never here be seen, oh!"

Lucie, knocked—once—twice, and interrupted the song. A little frightened voice called out "Who's that?"

Lucie opened the door: and what do you think there was inside the hill?—a nice clean kitchen with a flagged floor and wooden beams—just

like any other farm kitchen. Only the ceiling was so low that Lucie's head nearly touched it; and the pots and pans were small, and so was everything there.

There was a nice hot singey smell; and at the table, with an iron in her hand stood a very stout short person staring anxiously at Lucie.

Her print gown was tucked up, and she was wearing a large apron over her striped petticoat. Her little black nose went sniffle, sniffle, snuffle, and her eyes went twinkle, twinkle; and underneath her cap—where Lucie had yellow curls—that little person had PRICKLES!

"Who are you?" said Lucie. "Have you seen my pocket-handkins?"

The little person made a bob-curtsey—"Oh, yes, if you please'm; my name is Mrs. Tiggy-winkle; oh, yes if you please'm, I'm an excellent clearstarcher!" And she took something out of a clothes-basket, and spread it on the ironing-blanket.

"What's that thing?" said Lucie—"that's not my pocket-handkin?"

"Oh no, if you please'm; that's a little scarlet waistcoat belonging to Cock Robin!"

And she ironed it and folded it, and put it on one side.

Then she took something else off a clothes-horse—"That isn't my pinny?" said Lucie.

"Oh no, if you please'm; that's a damask table-cloth belonging to Jenny Wren; look how it's stained with currant wine! It's very bad to wash!" said Mrs. Tiggy-winkle.

Mrs. Tiggy-winkle's nose went sniffle, sniffle, snuffle, and her eyes went twinkle, twinkle; and she fetched another hot iron from the fire.

"There's one of my pocket-handkins!" cried Lucie—"and there's my pinny!"

Mrs. Tiggy-winkle ironed it, and goffered it, and shook out the frills.

"Oh that *is* lovely!" said Lucie.

"And what are those long yellow things with fingers like gloves?"

"Oh, that's a pair of stockings belonging to Sally Henny-penny—look how she's worn the heels out with scratching in the yard! She'll very soon go barefoot!" said Mrs. Tiggy-winkle.

"Why, there's another handkersniff—but it isn't mine; it's red?"

"Oh no, if you please'm; that one belongs to old Mrs. Rabbit; and it *did* so smell of onions! I've had to wash it separately, I can't get out the smell."

"There's another one of mine," said Lucie.

"What are those funny little white things?"

"That's a pair of mittens belonging to Tabby Kitten; I only have to iron them; she washes them herself."

"There's my last pocket-handkin!" said Lucie.

"And what are you dipping into the basin of starch?"

"They're little dicky shirt-fronts belonging to Tom Tit-mouse—most terrible particular!" said Mrs. Tiggy-winkle. "Now I've finished my ironing; I'm going to air some clothes."

"What are these dear soft fluffy things?" said Lucie.

"Oh those are woolly coats belonging to the little lambs at Skelghyl."

"Will their jackets take off?" asked Lucie.

"Oh yes, if you please'm; look at the sheep-mark on the shoulder. And here's one marked for Gatesgarth, and three that come from Little-town. They're *always* marked at washing!" said Mrs. Tiggy-winkle.

And she hung up all sorts and sizes of clothes—small brown coats of mice; and one velvety black mole-skin waistcoat; and a red tailcoat with no tail belonging to Squirrel Nutkin; and a very much shrunk blue jacket belonging to Peter Rabbit; and a petticoat, not marked, that had gone lost in the washing—and at last the basket was empty!

THE TALE OF MRS. TIGGY-WINKLE

Then Mrs. Tiggy-winkle made tea—a cup for herself and a cup for Lucie. They sat before the fire on a bench and looked sideways at one another. Mrs. Tiggy-winkle's hand, holding the tea-cup, was very very brown, and very very wrinkly with the soap-suds; and all through her gown and her cap, there were *hair-pins* sticking wrong end out; so that Lucie didn't like to sit too near her.

When they had finished tea, they tied up the clothes in bundles; and Lucie's pocket-handkerchiefs were folded up inside her clean pinny, and fastened with a silver safety-pin.

And then they made up the fire with turf, and came out and locked the door, and hid the key under the door-sill.

Then away down the hill trotted Lucie and Mrs. Tiggy-winkle with the bundles of clothes!

All the way down the path little animals came out of the fern to meet them; the very first that they met were Peter Rabbit and Benjamin Bunny!

And she gave them their nice clean clothes; and all the little animals and birds were so very much obliged to dear Mrs. Tiggy-winkle.

So that at the bottom of the hill when they came to the stile, there was nothing left to carry except Lucie's one little bundle.

THE TALE OF MRS. TIGGY-WINKLE

THE TALE OF MRS. TIGGY-WINKLE

Lucie scrambled up the stile with the bundle in her hand; and then she turned to say "Goodnight," and to thank the washer-woman—But what a *very* odd thing! Mrs. Tiggy-winkle had not waited either for thanks or for the washing bill!

She was running running running up the hill—and where was her white frilled cap? and her shawl? and her gown—and her petticoat?

THE TALE OF MRS. TIGGY-WINKLE

And *how* small she had grown—and *how* brown—and covered with PRICKLES!

Why! Mrs. Tiggy-winkle was nothing but a HEDGEHOG.

(Now some people say that little Lucie had been asleep upon the stile—but then how could she have found three clean pocket-handkins and a pinny, pinned with a silver safety-pin?

And besides—*I* have seen that door into the back of the hill called Cat Bells—and besides *I* am very well acquainted with dear Mrs. Tiggy-winkle!)

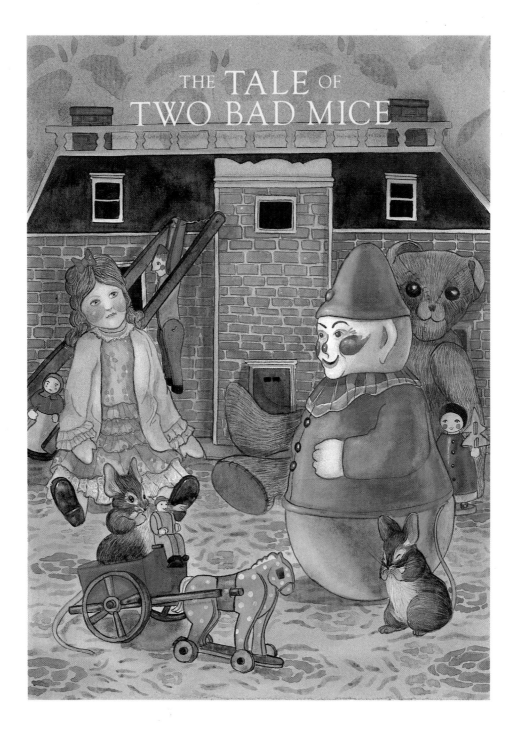

THE TALE OF
TWO BAD MICE

ONCE UPON A TIME there was a
very beautiful doll's-house; it was red brick with
white windows, and it had real muslin curtains and
a front door and a chimney.

It belonged to two Dolls called Lucinda and
Jane, at least it belonged to Lucinda, but she never
ordered meals.

Jane was the Cook; but she never did any
cooking, because the dinner had been bought ready-
made, in a box full of shavings.

THE TALE OF TWO BAD MICE

There were two red lobsters and a ham, a fish, a pudding, and some pears and oranges.

They would not come off the plates, but they were extremely beautiful.

One morning Lucinda and Jane had gone out for a drive in the doll's perambulator. There was no one in the nursery, and it was very quiet. Presently there was a little scuffling, scratching noise in a corner near the fire-place, where there was a hole under the skirting-board.

Tom Thumb put out his head for a moment, and then popped it in again.

Tom Thumb was a mouse.

A minute afterwards, Hunca Munca, his wife, put her head out, too; and when she saw that there was no one in the nursery, she ventured out on the oilcloth under the coalbox.

THE TALE OF TWO BAD MICE

THE TALE OF TWO BAD MICE

The doll's-house stood at the other side of the fire-place. Tom Thumb and Hunca Munca went cautiously across the hearthrug. They pushed the front door—it was not fast.

Tom Thumb and Hunca Munca went upstairs and peeped into the dining-room. Then they squeaked with joy!

Such a lovely dinner was laid out upon the table! There were tin spoons, and lead knives and forks, and two dolly-chairs— all *so* convenient!

Tom Thumb set to work at once to carve the ham. It was a beautiful shiny yellow, streaked with red.

The knife crumpled up and hurt him; he put his finger in his mouth.

"It is not boiled enough; it is hard. You have a try, Hunca Munca."

Hunca Munca stood up in her chair, and chopped at the ham with another lead knife.

"It's as hard as the hams at the cheesemonger's," said Hunca Munca.

The ham broke off the plate with a jerk, and rolled under the table.

"Let it alone," said Tom Thumb. "Give me some fish, Hunca Munca!"

Hunca Munca tried every tin spoon in turn; the fish was glued to the dish.

Then Tom Thumb lost his temper. He put the ham in the middle of the floor, and hit it with the tongs and with the shovel—bang, bang, smash, smash!

The ham flew all into pieces, for underneath the shiny paint it was made of nothing but plaster!

Then there was no end to the rage and disappointment of Tom Thumb and Hunca Munca. They broke up the pudding, the lobsters, the pears and the oranges.

As the fish would not come off the plate, they put it into the red-hot crinkly paper fire in the kitchen; but it would not burn either.

THE TALE OF TWO BAD MICE

THE TALE OF TWO BAD MICE

Tom Thumb went up the kitchen chimney and looked out at the top—there was no soot.

While Tom Thumb was up the chimney, Hunca Munca had another disappointment. She found some tiny canisters upon the dresser, labelled—Rice—Coffee—Sago—but when she turned them upside down, there was nothing inside except red and blue beads.

THE TALE OF TWO BAD MICE

Then those mice set to work to do all the mischief they could—especially Tom Thumb! He took Jane's clothes out of the chest of drawers in her bedroom, and he threw them out of the top floor window.

But Hunca Munca had a frugal mind. After pulling half the feathers out of Lucinda's bolster, she remembered that she herself was in want of a feather bed.

With Tom Thumb's assistance
she carried the bolster downstairs,
and across the hearthrug. It was
difficult to squeeze the bolster
into the mouse-hole; but they
managed it somehow.

Then Hunca Munca
went back and fetched a chair,
a book-case, a bird-cage, and
several small odds and ends.
The book-case and the bird-
cage refused to go into the
mouse-hole.

Hunca Munca left them behind the coal-box,
and went to fetch a cradle.

Hunca Munca was just
returning with another chair, when
suddenly there was a noise of
talking outside upon the landing.
The mice rushed back to their
hole, and the dolls came into
the nursery.

What a sight met the
eyes of Jane and Lucinda!

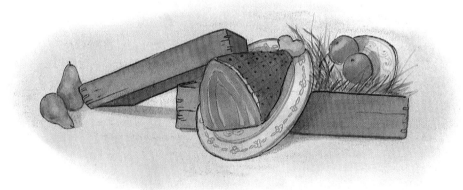

Lucinda sat upon the upset kitchen stove and stared; and Jane leant against the kitchen dresser and smiled—but neither of them made any remark.

THE TALE OF TWO BAD MICE

The book-case and the bird-cage were rescued from under the coal-box—but Hunca Munca has got the cradle, and some of Lucinda's clothes.

She also has some useful pots and pans, and several other things.

The little girl that the doll's-house belonged to said—"I will get a doll dressed like a policeman!"

But the nurse said—"I will set a mouse-trap!"

So that is the story of the two Bad Mice— but they were not so very very naughty after all, because Tom Thumb paid for everything he broke.

He found a crooked sixpence under the hearthrug; and upon Christmas Eve, he and Hunca Munca stuffed it into one of the stockings of Lucinda and Jane.

And very early every morning—before anybody is awake—Hunca Munca comes with her dust-pan and her broom to sweep the Dollies' house!

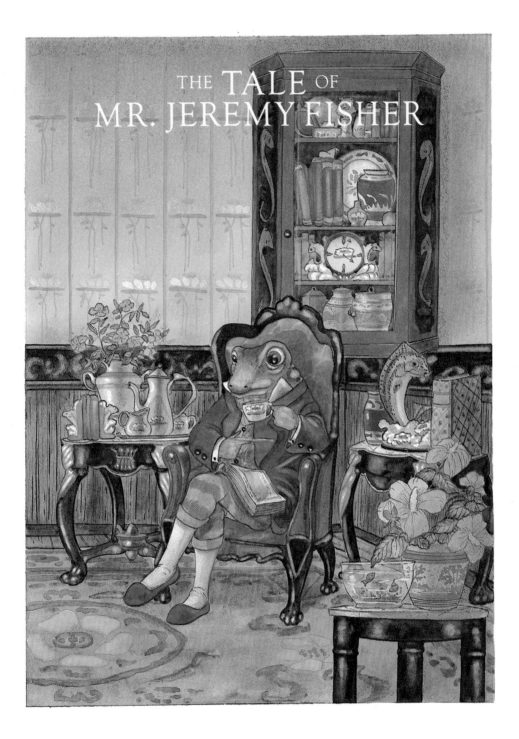

THE TALE OF
MR. JEREMY FISHER

ONCE UPON A TIME there was a frog
called Mr. Jeremy Fisher; he lived in a little damp
house amongst the buttercups at the edge of a pond.

The water was all slippy-sloppy in the larder
and in the back passage.

But Mr. Jeremy liked getting his feet wet;
nobody ever scolded him, and he never caught a
cold!

He was quite pleased when he looked out
and saw large drops of rain, splashing in the pond—

"I will get some worms and go fishing and
catch a dish of minnows for my dinner," said Mr.
Jeremy Fisher. "If I catch more than five fish, I will
invite my friends Mr. Alderman Ptolemy Tortoise
and Sir Isaac Newton. The Alderman, however, eats
salad."

THE TALE OF MR. JEREMY FISHER

Mr. Jeremy put on a macintosh, and a pair of shiny goloshes; he took his rod and basket, and set off with enormous hops to the place where he kept his boat.

The boat was round and green, and very like the other lily-leaves. It was tied to a water-plant in the middle of the pond.

Mr. Jeremy took a reed pole, and pushed the boat out into open water. "I know a good place for minnows," said Mr. Jeremy Fisher.

Mr. Jeremy stuck his pole into the mud and fastened his boat to it.

Then he settled himself cross-legged and
arranged his fishing tackle. He had the dearest
little red float. His rod was a tough stalk of
grass, his line was a fine long white horse-hair,
and he tied a little wriggling worm at the end.

The rain trickled down his back, and for
nearly an hour he stared at the float.

"This is getting tiresome, I think I should
like some lunch," said Mr. Jeremy Fisher.

He punted back again amongst the water-
plants, and took some lunch out of his basket.

"I will eat a butterfly sandwich, and wait till
the shower is over," said Mr. Jeremy Fisher.

A great big water-beetle came up underneath
the lily leaf and tweaked the toe of one of his
goloshes.

Mr. Jeremy crossed his legs up shorter, out of reach, and went on eating his sandwich.

Once or twice something moved about with a rustle and a splash amongst the rushes at the side of the pond.

"I trust that is not a rat," said Mr. Jeremy Fisher; "I think I had better get away from here."

Mr. Jeremy shoved the boat out again a little way, and dropped in the bait. There was a bite almost directly; the float gave a tremendous bobbit!

"A minnow! a minnow! I have him by the nose!" cried Mr. Jeremy Fisher, jerking up his rod.

THE TALE OF MR JEREMY FISHER

But what a horrible surprise! Instead of a smooth fat minnow, Mr. Jeremy landed little Jack Sharp the stickleback, covered with spines!

The stickleback floundered about the boat, pricking and snapping until he was quite out of breath. Then he jumped back into the water.

And a shoal of other little fishes put their heads out, and laughed at Mr. Jeremy Fisher.

And while Mr. Jeremy sat disconsolately on the edge of his boat—sucking his sore fingers and peering down into the water—a *much* worse thing happened; a really *frightful* thing it would have been, if Mr. Jeremy had not been wearing a macintosh!

A great big enormous trout came up—kerpflop-p-p-p! with a splash—and it seized Mr. Jeremy with a snap, "Ow! Ow! Ow!"—and then it turned and dived down to the bottom of the pond!

THE TALE OF MR. JEREMY FISHER

But the trout was so displeased with the taste of the macintosh, that in less than half a minute it spat him out again; and the only thing it swallowed was Mr. Jeremy's goloshes.

Mr. Jeremy bounced up to the surface of the water, like a cork and the bubbles out of a soda water bottle; and he swam with all his might to the edge of the pond.

He scrambled out on the first bank he came to, and he hopped home across the meadow with his macintosh all in tatters.

"What a mercy that was not a pike!" said Mr. Jeremy Fisher. "I have lost my rod and basket; but it does not much matter, for I am sure I should never have dared to go fishing again!"

THE TALE OF MR. JEREMY FISHER

He put some sticking plaster on his fingers, and his friends both came to dinner. He could not offer them fish, but he had something else in his larder.

Sir Isaac Newton wore his black and gold waistcoat, and Mr. Alderman Ptolemy Tortoise brought a salad with him in a string bag. And instead of a nice dish of minnows—they had a roasted grasshopper with lady-bird sauce; which frogs consider a beautiful treat; but *I* think it must have been nasty!

THE STORY OF MISS MOPPET

THIS IS A Pussy
called Miss Moppet,
she thinks she has heard
a mouse!

This is the Mouse
peeping out behind the
cupboard, and making
fun of Miss Moppet.
He is not afraid of a
kitten.

This is Miss
Moppet jumping just
too late; she misses
the Mouse and hits
her own head.
 She thinks it is
a very hard cupboard!
 The Mouse
watches Miss Moppet
from the top of the
cupboard.

THE STORY OF MISS MOPPET

Miss Moppet ties up her head in a duster, and sits before the fire.

The Mouse thinks she is looking very ill. He comes sliding down the bellpull.

THE STORY OF MISS MOPPET

Miss Moppet looks worse and worse. The Mouse comes a little nearer.

Miss Moppet holds her poor head in her paws, and looks at him through a hole in the duster. The Mouse comes *very* close.

THE STORY OF MISS MOPPET

And then all of a sudden—Miss Moppet
jumps upon the Mouse!

THE STORY OF MISS MOPPET

And because the Mouse has
teased Miss Moppet—Miss Moppet
thinks she will tease the Mouse;
which is not at all nice of Miss
Moppet.

She ties him up
in the duster, and
tosses it about like
a ball.

THE STORY OF MISS MOPPET

But she forgot about that hole in the duster; and when she untied it —there was no Mouse!

He has wriggled out and run away; and he is dancing a jig on the top of the cupboard!

THE TALE OF SQUIRREL NUTKIN

THIS IS A TALE about a tail—a tail that belonged to a little red squirrel, and his name was Nutkin.

He had a brother called Twinkleberry, and a great many cousins: they lived in a wood at the edge of a lake.

THE TALE OF SQUIRREL NUTKIN

In the middle of the lake there is an island covered with trees and nut bushes; and amongst those trees stands a hollow oak-tree, which is the house of an owl who is called Old Brown.

One autumn when the nuts were ripe, and the leaves on the hazel bushes were golden and green—Nutkin and Twinkleberry and all the other little squirrels came out of the wood, and down to the edge of the lake.

They made little rafts out of twigs, and they paddled away over the water to Owl Island to gather nuts.

Each squirrel had a little sack and a large oar, and spread out his tail for a sail.

They also took with them an offering of three fat mice as a present for Old Brown, and put them down upon his door-step.

Then Twinkleberry and the other little squirrels each made a low bow, and said politely—

"Old Mr. Brown, will you favour us with permission to gather nuts upon your island?"

But Nutkin was excessively impertinent in his manners. He bobbed up and down like a little red *cherry*, singing—

"Riddle me, riddle me, rot-tot-tote!
 A little wee man, in a red red coat!
 A staff in his hand, and a stone in his throat;
 If you'll tell me this riddle, I'll give you a groat."

Now this riddle is as old as the hills; Mr. Brown paid no attention whatever to Nutkin.

He shut his eyes obstinately and went to sleep.

The squirrels filled their little sacks with nuts, and sailed away home in the evening.

But next morning they all came back again to Owl Island; and Twinkleberry and the others brought a fine fat mole, and laid it on the stone in front of Old Brown's doorway, and said—

"Mr. Brown, will you favour us with your gracious permission to gather some more nuts?"

But Nutkin, who had no respect, began to dance up and down, tickling old Mr. Brown with a *nettle* and singing—

"Old Mr. B! Riddle-me-ree!
  Hitty Pitty within the wall,
  Hitty Pitty without the wall;
  If you touch Hitty Pitty,
  Hitty Pitty will bite you!"

Mr. Brown woke up suddenly and carried the mole into his house.

He shut the door in Nutkin's face. Presently a little thread of blue *smoke* from a wood fire came up from the top of the tree, and Nutkin peeped through the key-hole and sang—

"A house full, a hole full!
  And you cannot gather a bowl-full!"

The squirrels searched for nuts all over the island and filled their little sacks.

But Nutkin gathered oak-apples—yellow and scarlet—and sat upon a beech-stump playing marbles, and watching the door of old Mr. Brown.

THE TALE OF SQUIRREL NUTKIN

THE TALE OF SQUIRREL NUTKIN

On the third day the squirrels got
up very early and went fishing; they caught
seven fat minnows as a present for Old Brown.

They paddled over the lake and landed
under a crooked chest-nut tree on Owl Island.

Twinkleberry and six other little squirrels
each carried a fat minnow; but Nutkin, who had no
nice manners, brought no present at all. He ran in
front, singing—

"The man in the wilderness said to me,
'How many strawberries grow in the sea?'
I answered him as I thought good—
'As many red herrings as grow in the wood.'"

But old Mr. Brown took no interest in
riddles—not even when the answer was provided for
him.

On the fourth day the squirrels brought a
present of six fat beetles, which were as good as

plums in *plum-pudding* for Old Brown. Each beetle was wrapped up carefully in a dock-leaf, fastened with a pine-needle pin.

But Nutkin sang as rudely as ever—

"Old Mr. B! riddle-me-ree
Flour of England, fruit of Spain,
Met together in a shower of rain;
Put in a bag tied round with a string,
If you'll tell me this riddle, I'll give you a ring!"

Which was ridiculous of Nutkin, because he had not got any ring to give to Old Brown.

The other squirrels hunted up and down the nut bushes; but Nutkin gathered robin's pin-cushions off a briar bush, and stuck them full of pine-needle pins.

On the fifth day the squirrels brought a present of wild honey; it was so sweet and sticky that they licked their fingers as they put it down

THE TALE OF SQUIRREL NUTKIN

upon the stone. They had stolen it out of a
bumble *bees'* nest on the tippitty top of
the hill.

But Nutkin skipped up and down,
singing—
"Hum-a-bum! buzz! buzz! Hum-a-bum buzz!
    As I went over Tipple-tine
    I met a flock of bonny swine;
Some yellow-nacked, some yellow backed!
    They were the very bonniest swine
    That e'er went over Tipple-tine."

Old Mr. Brown turned up his eyes in disgust
at the impertinence of Nutkin.

But he ate up the honey!

The squirrels filled their little sacks with nuts.

But Nutkin sat upon a big flat rock and
played ninepins with a crab apple and green fircones.

THE TALE OF SQUIRREL NUTKIN

THE TALE OF SQUIRREL NUTKIN

THE TALE OF SQUIRREL NUTKIN

On the sixth day, which was Saturday, the squirrels came again for the last time; they brought a new-laid *egg* in a little rush basket as a last parting present for Old Brown.

But Nutkin ran in front laughing, and shouting—

"Humpty Dumpty lies in the beck,
With a white counterpane round his neck,
Forty doctors and forty wrights,
Cannot put Humpty Dumpty to rights!"

Now old Mr. Brown took an interest in eggs; he opened one eye and shut it again. But still he did not speak.

Nutkin became more and more impertinent—

THE TALE OF SQUIRREL NUTKIN

"Old Mr. B! Old Mr. B!
Hickamore, Hackamore, on
   the King's kitchen door;
All the King's horses, and
   all the King's men,
Couldn't drive Hickamore,
   Hackamore,
Off the King's kitchen
   door."

    Nutkin danced
up and down like a
sunbeam; but still
Old Brown said
nothing at all.

THE TALE OF SQUIRREL NUTKIN

Nutkin began again—

"Arthur O'Bower has broken his band,
He comes roaring up the land!
The King of Scots with all his power,
Cannot turn Arthur of the Bower!"

Nutkin made a whirring noise to sound like the *wind*, and he took a running jump right onto the head of Old Brown! ...

Then all at once there was a flutterment and a scufflement and a loud "Squeak!"

The other squirrels scuttered away into the bushes.

When they came back very cautiously, peeping round the tree—there was Old Brown sitting on his door-step, quite still, with his eyes closed, as if nothing had happened.

THE TALE OF SQUIRREL NUTKIN

*   *   *   *   *

But Nutkin was in his waistcoat pocket!

This looks like the end of the story; but it isn't.

Old Brown carried Nutkin into his house, and held him up by the tail, intending to skin him; but Nutkin pulled so very hard that his tail broke in two, and he dashed up the staircase and escaped out of the attic window.

And to this day, if you meet Nutkin up a tree and ask him a riddle, he will throw sticks at you and stamp his feet and scold, and shout—

"Cuck-cuck-cuck-cur-r-r-cuck-k-k!"

A

PPLEY DAPPLY,
a little brown mouse,
Goes to the cupboard in somebody's house.

APPLEY DAPPLY'S NURSERY RHYMES

In somebody's cupboard
      there's everything nice,
Cake, cheese, jam, biscuits,
      —All charming for mice!

Appley Dapply has little
      sharp eyes,
And Appley Dapply is *so* fond
      of pies!

Now who
is this knocking
at Cotton-tail's door?
Tap tappit! Tap tappit!
She's heard it before?

And when she peeps out
    there is nobody there,
But a present of carrots
    put down on
    the stair.

Hark! I hear it again!
    Tap, tap, tappit! Tap tappit!
Why—I really believe it's a
    little black rabbit!

O LD
Mr. Pricklepin
has never a cushion to
stick his pins in,
His nose is black and his
beard is gray,
And he lives in an ash stump
over the way.

YOU KNOW
the old woman
who lived in a shoe?
And had so many children
She didn't know what to do?

I think if she lived in
a little shoe-house—
That little old woman was
surely a mouse!

D

IGGORY
Diggory Delvet!
A little old man in black velvet;
He digs and he delves—
You can see for yourselves
The mounds dug by Diggory Delvet.

G RAVY

and potatoes
in a good brown pot—

Put them in the oven,
and serve them very hot!

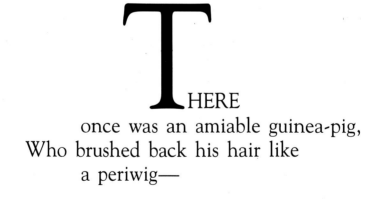

THERE
once was an amiable guinea-pig,
Who brushed back his hair like
a periwig—

He wore a sweet tie,
as blue as the sky—
And his whiskers and buttons
were very big.

THE TALE OF
BENJAMIN BUNNY

ONE MORNING a little rabbit sat on a bank.

He pricked his ears and listened to the trit-trot, trit-trot of a pony.

A gig was coming along the road; it was driven by Mr. McGregor, and beside him sat Mrs. McGregor in her best bonnet.

As soon as they had passed, little Benjamin Bunny slid down into the road, and set off— with a hop, skip and a jump—to call upon his relations, who lived in the wood at the back of Mr. McGregor's garden.

THE TALE OF BENJAMIN BUNNY

That wood was full of rabbit holes; and in the neatest sandiest hole of all, lived Benjamin's aunt and his cousins—Flopsy, Mopsy, Cotton-tail and Peter.

Old Mrs. Rabbit was a widow; she earned her living by knitting rabbit-wool mittens and muffetees

(I once bought a pair at a bazaar). She also sold herbs, and rosemary tea, and rabbit-tobacco (which is what *we* call lavender).

Little Benjamin did not very much want to see his Aunt.

He came round the back of the fir-tree, and nearly tumbled upon the top of his Cousin Peter.

Peter was sitting by himself. He looked poorly, and was dressed in a red cotton pocket-handkerchief.

"Peter"—said little Benjamin, in a whisper— "who has got your clothes?"

Peter replied—"The scare-crow in Mr. McGregor's garden," and described how he had been chased about the garden, and had dropped his shoes and coat.

Little Benjamin sat down beside his cousin, and assured him that Mr. McGregor had gone out in a gig, and Mrs. McGregor also; and certainly for the day, because she was wearing her best bonnet.

Peter said he hoped that it would rain.

At this point, old Mrs. Rabbit's voice was heard inside the rabbit hole, calling—"Cotton-tail! Cotton-tail! fetch some more camomile!"

Peter said he thought he might feel better if he went for a walk.

THE TALE OF BENJAMIN BUNNY

They went away hand in hand, and got upon the flat top of the wall at the bottom of the wood. From here they looked down into Mr. McGregor's garden. Peter's coat and shoes were plainly to be seen upon the scare-crow, topped with an old tam-o-shanter of Mr. McGregor's.

Little Benjamin said, "It spoils people's clothes to squeeze under a gate; the proper way to get in, is to climb down a pear-tree."

Peter fell down head first; but it was of no consequence, as the bed below was newly raked and quite soft.

It had been sown with lettuces.

THE TALE OF BENJAMIN BUNNY

They left a great many odd little foot-marks all over the bed, especially little Benjamin, who was wearing clogs.

Little Benjamin said that the first thing to be done was to get back Peter's clothes, in order that they might be able to use the pocket-handkerchief.

They took them off the scare-crow. There had been rain during the night; there was water in the shoes, and the coat was somewhat shrunk.

133

Benjamin tried on the tam-o-shanter, but it was too big for him.

Then he suggested that they should fill the pocket-handkerchief with onions, as a little present for his Aunt.

Peter did not seem to be enjoying himself; he kept hearing noises.

Benjamin, on the contrary, was perfectly at home, and ate a lettuce leaf. He said that he was in the habit of coming to the garden with his father to get lettuces for their Sunday dinner.

(The name of little Benjamin's papa was old Mr. Benjamin Bunny.)

The lettuces certainly were very fine.

Peter did not eat anything; he said he should like to go home. Presently he dropped half the onions.

Little Benjamin said that it was not possible to get back up the pear-tree, with a load of vegetables. He led the way boldly towards the other end of the garden. They went along a little walk on planks, under a sunny red-brick wall.

The mice sat on their door-steps cracking cherry-stones, they winked at Peter Rabbit and little Benjamin Bunny.

Presently Peter let the pocket-handkerchief go again.

They got amongst flower-pots, and frames and tubs; Peter heard noises worse than ever, his eyes were as big as lolly-pops!

He was a step or two in front of his cousin, when he suddenly stopped.

THE TALE OF BENJAMIN BUNNY

This is what those little rabbits saw round that corner!

Little Benjamin took one look, and then, in half a minute less than no time, he hid himself and Peter and the onions underneath a large basket....

The cat got up and stretched herself, and came and sniffed at the basket.

Perhaps she liked the smell of onions!

Anyway, she sat down upon the top of the basket.

She sat there for
five hours.

THE TALE OF BENJAMIN BUNNY

* * * * *
I cannot draw you
a picture of Peter and
Benjamin underneath
the basket, because it
was quite dark, and
because the smell of
onions was fearful;
it made Peter
Rabbit and little
Benjamin cry.

The sun got
round
behind
the wood,
and it was quite
late in the afternoon; but still
the cat sat upon the basket.
At length there was a
pitter-patter, pitter-patter,
and some bits of
mortar fell from the
wall above.

THE TALE OF BENJAMIN BUNNY

THE TALE OF BENJAMIN BUNNY

The cat looked up and saw old Mr. Benjamin Bunny prancing along the top of the wall of the upper terrace.

He was smoking a pipe of rabbit-tobacco, and had a little switch in his hand.

He was looking for his son.

Old Mr. Bunny had no opinion whatever of cats.

He took a tremendous jump off the top of the wall on to the top of the cat, and cuffed it off the basket, and kicked it into the green-house, scratching off a handful of fur.

The cat was too much surprised to scratch back.

When old Mr. Bunny had driven the cat into the green-house, he locked the door.

Then he came back to the basket and took out his son Benjamin by the ears, and whipped him with the little switch.

Then he took out his nephew Peter.

Then he took out the handkerchief of onions, and marched out of the garden.

When Mr. McGregor returned about half an hour later, he observed several things which perplexed him.

It looked as though some person had been walking all over the garden in a pair of clogs—only the foot-marks were too ridiculously little!

Also he could not understand how the cat could have managed to shut herself up *inside* the green-house, locking the door upon the *outside*.

THE TALE OF BENJAMIN BUNNY

When Peter got home, his mother forgave him, because she was so glad to see that he had found his shoes and coat. Cotton-tail and Peter folded up the pocket-handkerchief, and old Mrs. Rabbit strung up the onions and hung them from the kitchen ceiling, with the bunches of herbs and the rabbit-tobacco.

ILLUSTRATOR'S NOTE

I can remember sitting on my bed as a child, listening to my mother read Beatrix Potter's THE TALE OF PETER RABBIT. She read and re-read this story to me until I was old enough to pick up the book for myself. I quickly moved on to read all the other wonderful Potter stories, such as THE TAILOR OF GLOUCESTER, THE TALE OF MRS. TIGGY-WINKLE, and THE TALE OF BENJAMIN BUNNY, to name a few. The daring exploits of Peter and Benjamin made me yearn for this kind of adventure. Before long, I was sneaking into my next-door neighbor's backyard and helping myself—in this case to apples, not lettuce.

There is a tremendous warmth and affection one feels reading these stories that carries over time after time. It comes through in THE TAILOR OF GLOUCESTER, when the mice help their friend, the ailing tailor, finish sewing the Mayor's jacket on time, and in THE TALE OF BENJAMIN BUNNY, when Benjamin tries on Mr. McGregor's oversized tam. Above all, it is this generous spirit along with the spare beauty of the Potter drawings that makes these tales classic.

My taste in art runs from Potter's seeming effortlessness (and I emphasize "seeming") to the watercolor fantasy worlds of Edmund Dulac, Aubrey Beardsley, and Arthur Rackham. Although each of these artists is unique, there is one thing they all have in common: each has created a distinctive and memorable visual world. It is for this reason that I wanted to illustrate the stories that make up this volume—to have an excuse (though one is not really needed) to return once more to the delightful world of Beatrix Potter, which I hope I shall never altogether put behind me.

I was reluctant at first to consider the prospect of illustrating a new edition of PETER RABBIT. The temptation to give the stories a new rendering and the sheer pleasure of spending time in Peter's world eventually overcame my doubts. I have tried not to copy Miss Potter's illustrations, nor to bring a contemporary look to the characters, but to retain the original spirit in my own interpretations.

For these illustrations, I began with a rough thumbnail sketch to try to get the characters just right. This was followed by a larger, full-sized rough pencil drawing in which I started to put in background and details. I moved on to a finished pencil drawing from which I painted, first laying down either a warm or cool unifying base color. Next, I layered the watercolors, one on top of the other, to build up a specific color. Lastly, I did the line work in order to give the picture a softer overall look. For the finished pencils, I used a 2H lead pencil sharpened to a needle point. For the brushes, I used everything from a .0000 for the fine detail work to a #8 for the backgrounds.

ALLEN ATKINSON

This book was set in Goudy Old Style and composed by TypoGraphics Communications, Inc., New York, New York. Printed and bound by W. A. Krueger Co., New Berlin, Wisconsin. Color separations by Toppan Printing Co. (America) Inc., New York, New York.

Designer: Iris Bass
Art Director: Armand Eisen
Editorial Production: John Woodside
Production: Ellen McNeilly